Copyright © 2001 by Nord-Süd Verlag AG, Gossau Zürich, Switzerland
First published in Switzerland under the title *Frohe Ostern! Pauli*
English translation copyright © 2001 by North-South Books, Inc.

First published in the United States, Great Britain, Canada, Australia, and New Zealand in 2001
by North-South Books, an imprint of Nord-Süd Verlag AG, Gossau Zürich, Switzerland
Distributed in the United States by North-South Books Inc., New York

Library of Congress Cataloging-in-Publication Data is available.
The CIP catalogue record for this book is available from The British Library.

ISBN 0-7358-1436-8 (trade) 10 9 8 7 6 5 4 3 2 1
ISBN 0-7358-1437-6 (library) 10 9 8 7 6 5 4 3 2 1
Printed in Belgium

For more information about our books, and the authors and artists
who create them, visit our web site: www.northsouth.com

Happy Easter, Davy!

Brigitte Weninger
Illustrated by Eve Tharlet
Translated by Rosemary Lanning

A MICHAEL NEUGEBAUER BOOK

NORTH-SOUTH BOOKS / NEW YORK / LONDON

Spring had come at last! Davy, the little rabbit,
and his family sat outside their burrow, soaking up
the warm sunshine.
Suddenly, Davy's big brother Dan came running.

"Guess what I've just heard," said Dan, excitedly.
"Tomorrow is Easter, when human children
get presents and pretty eggs. And who
brings them? A rabbit! He's
called the Easter Bunny, and he
lives right here in this wood!"
"Where?" asked Davy.
Father Rabbit scratched his head. "There are lots of rabbits
in the wood," he said, "but I've never met an Easter Bunny."

"Me want present!" squeaked baby Dinah.

"Me too," said big sister Daisy. "Why doesn't he bring us anything?"

"Let's go and ask him," said Donny.

So off they went to find the Easter Bunny.

They searched high and low,
but the Easter Bunny was
nowhere to be found.

Davy's brothers and sisters went home, disappointed,
but Davy stayed behind to think.
"It's not fair," he grumbled to Nicky, his toy rabbit.
"The Easter Bunny should come to us. We're bunnies!"

Suddenly Davy jumped up.
"I've got an idea!" he said.
"Come on, Nicky. We've
got work to do."

"First we need some eggs," said Davy. "I wonder
where the Easter Bunny gets them?" He saw a nest
with five speckled eggs, but he couldn't take those.
There were baby birds inside, waiting to hatch. Davy
ran down to the riverbank and found some beautiful,
egg-shaped pebbles instead.
"Now for the presents," he said.

Davy found a secret place to work all day long.
First he painted the pebbles. Then he made a basket
for Daisy's toys, an Easter Bunny doll for little Dinah,
and bark boats for Dan and Donny.
"Finished at last, Nicky!" he said. "Tomorrow everyone
will think the Easter Bunny came after all!"

That night, Davy was so excited he could hardly sleep.
When dawn broke he tiptoed outside and hid the eggs and
presents. His brothers and sisters were still fast asleep when
he crept back into bed.

At last the rabbit children woke up and hopped out of the burrow. Daisy tripped over something round.

"Look! I've found an Easter egg!" she cried.

"And here's another one!" said Dan. "So the Easter Bunny did come!" Daisy, Donny, Dinah, and Dan started an egg hunt. They were so excited when they found all the other eggs, and the presents!

"What about you, Davy?" said Mother Rabbit. "Didn't you find anything?" Davy blushed from head to toe.

Now they would all guess that he was the Easter Bunny!
"N-n-not yet," he stammered.

Davy pretended to look under a bush.
He knew he hadn't hidden anything there.

But what was this?
A pretty painted egg and a little wooden flute.
Davy was puzzled. Who
could have hidden them?

"How nice," said Father Rabbit. "It seems the kind Easter Bunny
brought something for all our children! This calls for a celebration.
Let's have a picnic!"

So the rabbit family spent a happy Easter day out in the meadow.

And the happiest of all was Davy, the secret Easter Bunny!